Drowning Rain

A Novel

Alan Welker

· RainierGate ·

First Edition
Graphics & Photography by Alan Welker

Dedication ◆

Suzanne, my love, you make me so proud every single day and I promise forever and ever...

Life

View from Fourth & Spring, Seattle, WA

"You gave me life, now show me how to live."

Audioslave
Show Me How to Live

Chapter 1

Familiar, mundane, and routine – such were the days of my life until...

I was awakened every morning at 6:30 by the sound of *The BJ Shea Experience* on KISW – 99.9FM. I was awakened every morning and headed straight to the bathroom. I was awakened every morning and poured myself a bowl of Cheerios and skim milk. I was awakened every morning to a fifteen minute commute. I was awakened every morning to another day unlived, unappreciated, and unsung. I was awakened every morning, but never awoke at all.

Days, weeks, even months went by without notice. Each day I went to the same job, sat in the same cubical, and stared at the same screen for eight hours – eight hours minus an hour lunch, minus gossiping around the water-cooler, minus refilling a stained mug with a stale, bitter blend, minus staring blankly at colorless tiles while listening to the roaring drain, minus standing shoulder-to-shoulder on the ride down with muted co-workers as the monotone music played.

Familiar, mundane, and routine – such were the days of my life until that February afternoon. It was 11:30 – time for lunch. I emerged from the elevator as part of the herd and was headed to the cafeteria food-court located on the ground floor. I emerged from the elevator as part of the herd and made a beeline towards

Panda Express for a bowl of Orange Chicken with steamed rice. I emerged from the elevator as part of the herd and followed the collage of the well-groomed, generically-styled. I emerged from the elevator as part of the herd and then...

"Oh my God! He's got a gun!"

It was Randle Keggin. He was a nice guy. A good guy. Kind of shy, but he came around after awhile. He loved talking about his kids, all three of them. The way he told it, they were perfect angels – every one. Sandy, his oldest, just got accepted to Seattle Pacific University. His son Daniel broke the school record for most sacks in a game. Then there was Blake, their little surprise after 22-years-of-marriage. He just turned one the week before and Randle threw a barbeque – invited everyone from the office. I went.

The beer was cold, the burgers were hot, and the cake was good too. Even his wife wasn't as bitchy as usual. What really got me though was the look on that kid's face when he saw what I got him – priceless.

I had no idea what to get the little tyke. Never shopped for a one-year-old before, so I decided to play it safe and got the kid a giant stuffed teddy-bear. From the looks of his father though, I should have gotten him some body-armor; poor kid.

Okay, that was unfair. I don't mean to imply that Randle would hurt his family. Actually, I've never seen so much as a hint of violence from ol' Randle before he pulled that gun, but situations have a way of changing people. And with the situation poor Randle found himself in... Well, I can't blame him for going a little nuts.

A week after Emerald International posted record earnings, the pink-slips went out. The powers that be on the 32nd Floor decided to move the entire R and D Department (that's Research and Development) to Singapore. And who do you think was one of the unlucky software engineers on the receiving end? You guessed it.

I like to think I kind of knew how he felt. Sure, I didn't get a pick-slip; they just transferred me to Accounts Payable. And sure, I didn't have a wife or kids or really anyone to take care of besides myself. Still, I'm kind of a sensitive person and I could really emphasis with his plight. It bothered me. It really bothered me.

"Drop it!"

Nathan Tosh to the rescue. What an idiot. And the most arrogant man I've ever met. Thinks he's God's gift to women. Told me one time he got mistaken for Johnny Depp. And to be fair, I see the resemblance – if Johnny got ran over by a street-sweeper.

Yeah, it may seem like I'm being unduly harsh on Nathan and maybe that's true, but I lost all respect for the guy after I found out why he got kicked off the police force. Get this, a couple of years ago he was giving a talk over gun safety at Bailey Gatzert Elementary up on Yesler when, for reasons only known to him, he decided to pass a loaded service pistol around to the students. One kid thought it was a toy and shot himself in the leg. Of course, Nathan maintains that he thought the gun wasn't loaded, like that really changes anything. He could have killed somebody. Ironically, it was him that stood between us and Randle's semi-automatic.

Chapter 2 ◊

Things didn't fair too well for ol' Randle. Before he even knew what was going on, Nathan shot him in the back of the head. Of course, he wasn't the only one that had a bad day.

Debbie Jacobs, a secretary from the third floor, just happened to be in the wrong place at the wrong time. After passing through Randle's skull, the .44 caliber round struck Debbie in the abdomen and got lodged in her spine. She'll never walk again.

To tell you the truth, I didn't really

feel too sorry for her. She was one of those brainless, prissy bitches that are so popular these days: blond hair, blue eyes, huge fake tits. You know, the typical office skank. Besides, she got a huge settlement out of whole thing.

Nathan was let go after the incident. His whole shoot-first-and-ask-questions-later routine didn't sit too well with the executives at Emerald International. Instead of labeling him a hero, they made him out to be Dirty Harry. Granted, he carried the same sidearm, but the similarities really end there. As much as I hate the guy, I have to admit he probably saved lives that day. Who knows what the hell Randle was going to do?

Anyway, about a week and a half later on Saturday, there were services held for Randle - closed casket of course. It was amazing how many people showed up. Even Debbie was there in her new electric wheelchair.

I know it's wrong but, when I saw her, the jingle from the old Power Wheels commercials played in my head. *Pow. Pow. Pow. Power Wheels. Pow. Power Wheels. Now I'm driving for real!*

His family, oh my God, they were in shock. Just in absolute shock. Then again, I think everybody was. A person was dead, another was paralyzed, and for what? What was the cause of it all?

I'll tell you. It was the executives at Emerald International. If those bastards up on the 32nd floor cared about the people that work for them half as much as the bottom-line, none of this would have happened. Take people's jobs and ship them overseas, how the hell do they expect people to react? It's not like people can just go out and get another job, not with the economy the way is; nobody's hiring. Then you have a poor bastard like Randle with a kid headed to college, a baby to take care of, and another one in high school. Is it any wonder why things turned out the way they had?

I sat there in the small, stuffy chapel watching the gathering and the rituals of mourning. I sat there in silence, thinking. I sat there, assigning blame.

"Hell of a thing, isn't it?"

It was none other than Prudence Baker – everyone called her Prue. Prue Baker. She was the petite raven-haired goddess that served as our office receptionist. There was something about her, something that drove me wild. Maybe it was her smile. Maybe it was her heir of playful mischievousness. Maybe it was her deep hazel eyes. Maybe it was her soft, milky complexion. Maybe it was slender frame. Maybe it was her firm, perky breasts. Whatever it was, I wanted her. I wanted her from the first moment I laid eyes on her. How often I thought and wondered what she would feel like. What would she taste like? What sounds would she make? How often I fantasized about taking her on the copier, in the breakroom, right at her desk with everyone watching, but I never had the nerve to even ask her out.

Part of the reason I never asked her out was the fact that she was a co-worker. If it didn't work out, things could get awkward. I'd have to see her everyday. You know, that whole don't-shit-where-you-eat kind of thing.

So, there was that, and I didn't really know if she was available. Maybe she was seeing someone. Maybe she already had a man in her life. Maybe she was adept at munching carpet. At the viewing though, she was by herself. No one was with her. It was finally apparent, she was alone.

Of course, there was another reason. A reason under most circumstances I'd never admit; however, for you I'll make an exception. I'm pretty sure I can trust you. The reason was fear, plain and simple. I wasn't afraid of her mind you, but the idea of putting myself out there. It was a pathological fear of rejection accompanied by the questions – the endless, unbearable questions. How would she react? What would she say? Would she turn me down?

"Huh? Oh, yeah. Yeah, just terrible."

"Terrible," Prue repeated. "So, how you holdin' up? I know you guys were close."

We were close? Where did she get that idea? "Umm, I'm doing alright. You know, as good as to be expected I guess."

"Well, good. Let me know if you need anything. I'm here for you."

"Well..."

"What is it?"

"No, it's nothing."

"No, what is it?"

"Well..."

"Yeah."

"I could use a good screw right about now."

"Really? Then by all means, take me now you inglorious bastard," Prue cried as she threw herself into my waiting arms.

Okay, I made up that last little bit. Just seeing if you're awake and paying attention. The conversation actually ended with the usual clichéd gestures and pleasantries after she made it known that she was there for me.

I felt good. I felt really good. She liked me. It was clear Prue liked me. And for a moment, I let my mind wander to places only accessible through hope. Still, all too quickly, I realized where I was and I became acutely aware of the irony of being in such a state on such an inauspicious occasion.

What would they say? What would they think if they saw me sitting there all starry-eyed with a grin on my face? And with that, I suppressed all outward showing of emotion – masked it with a grim, grave face. No one would be the wiser. No one would suspect I was in love.

Chapter 3 ♦

I hadn't always been such a fine upstanding citizen: going to work in a suit and tie, giving to various charitable organizations, occasionally going to mass. For a time, for a long time, I lived in the sands and hyper-lucid reality of Venice Beach, California. I went there to find myself – to loose myself. I accomplished both, but I traded that life in for the stability and predictability that can only be found when your world is limited to a cubical. Of course, I see now that the predictability and seeming banality is nothing more than a façade – a thin, cheap mask over the face of chaos.

It was my last day at Emerald International, but I was the only one who knew it. After everything that happened, I just couldn't bring myself to stay there. I felt... I guess I felt betrayed in a way. Nothing seemed quite right. Nothing seemed real.

At the time, I wasn't sure what I was going to do. Maybe go back to school. Maybe do a little writing. Maybe go work for my friend Jess Garrett down at his bookstore – Garrett's Books.

Jess and I went way back. I mean way back. We grew up together down in Olympia - lived right across the street from each other and we had some pretty good times. Our neighborhood was right behind LP Brown Elementary, so we'd always be over there playing catch, messing around on the jungle-gym, riding our bikes through the woods. Yeah, we hung out from elementary all the way up to high school. Both played football for Capital. Then, during our Sophomore year, his dad got a job up in Bellingham and that was it. I mean, we kept in-touch for awhile, but you know how it is. Anyway, years later, I had just started at Emerald International and was out for a little stroll during lunch when I decided to pop into this neat little bookstore. Found out Jess owned the place. He had just inherited it from his grandfather not two-months before. Since then, we hung out off and on. Of course, he has a wife and two spoiled brats, so it's kind of hard to make time.

Anyway, it was my last day at Emerald International and I was determined to make the most of it. That meant grabbing as much office supplies as I could get my hands on, telling my boss to go fuck himself, and asking Prue out to dinner - not necessarily in that order. On the way to work, however, I had a little change of plans - keep it simple. I decided to go about my day as usual, not tell anyone I was leaving, and just ask Prue out.

When I walked in, Prue was at her desk wearing a sleeveless black dress with a gold chain and her hair tucked neatly in a ponytail.

Hey there, Beautiful. "Good morning, Prue."

"Aw, good morning. How you holdin' up?"

"I'm doin' alright, I guess."

"Yeah?"

"You know. Takin' it one day at a time."

"Well, that's good."

"Yeah, well…"

"Yeah?"

"I was wonderin' if you didn't have plans later, maybe we could go grab a bite to eat." *Smooth.*

"Uh... Yeah, I could do that. What were you thinking?"

Oh my God, she said yes. "Do you like the Hard Rock Café?"

"Oh, I've been dying to try that place!"

"Great. Meet there at eight?"

"Sounds good."

"Alright. Well, have a good day."

"You too."

I practically floated to my desk. I was on cloud nine. Nothing could bring me down. That is, nothing but Stanley Henderson.

Stanley Henderson – I hate even writing his name. You may think your boss is an asshole but, trust me, they have nothing on Stanley; he's in a class by himself. If I ever went off and starting taking people out, ol' Stanley would be right at the top of the list.

Almost every time I saw that gelatinous blob, I would fantasize about something or other. It became my way of coping with the asshole. Typically, I thought about pressing a gun to his head and forcing him to eat that decaying rat carcass he calls a toupee. During department meetings, while he'd endlessly prattle on-and-on about nothing, I often thought about getting him alone and playing dissection with a large hunting knife – forcing his still pulsating heart down his throat. Of course, there was the Christmas party a couple of years ago when it was my turn to host. I thought about adding a rather generous amount of Orange Glo to his screwdriver.

Did I mention I hate the guy?

"You're late."

"I know. I think I might be

pregnant."

"Oh hardy, har, har. That's so hilarious. Everything's just a big freaking joke to you isn't it? You've been late twice this week. And, instead of apologizing, what do you do?"

"You know what? You're right. You're right and I'm sorry."

"Well, that's better."

"I'm sorry you're such an anal-retentive prick."

"What?!" Stanley stammered.

"I'm sorry you can't get laid because women would rather resort to bestiality than be with you."

"Where in the hell do you get off?!"

"And I'm sorry I didn't do this sooner," I sprang up from my office chair and got right in his pudgy, acne scarred face. "I quit!"

Chapter 4 ◆

Standing outside of the Hard Rock Café at the Pike Place Market, I glanced down and looked at my watch – 7:54pm. When I looked up, I caught sight of Prue crossing in front of City Target.

"Waiting long?" she asked, adjusting the purse strap on her shoulder.

"No, just got here and put my name in," I paused as our eyes met. "You look amazing."

"I know," she replied with a grin.

I smiled.

"So, how long of a wait do we have?"

Prue continued.

"Hostess said it should be about twenty minutes."

"Screw that. Let's just go find a place at the bar."

"Good idea," I replied, pulling open the door.

"What a gentleman."

Inside the atmosphere was warm and inviting. The air was rich with the aroma of burgers and beer. Centered over the bar was a television set playing the video of *Sex and Candy* by Marcy Playground. Luckily, we found two empty stools side-by-side at the end of the bar.

I helped Prue off with her jacket and carefully draped it over the back of her stool.

"What can I start you off with?" a tall redhead dressed in a black Hard Rock tee asked as I took a seat.

"Menus," I responded.

"Anything to drink?" She responded, handing us a menu each from behind the bar.

"Guinness."

"And for you?"

"I'll just have a Coke," Prue replied.

"Alright," the bartender smiled.

"What are you getting?" Prue asked after a few moments.

"I'm thinking the Classic Burger," I replied, setting down the menu.

"Can't go wrong with that," Prue grinned.

Just then, the bartender returned with our drinks. "Ready to order?"

"Yeah, I'll have the Classic Burger," Prue replied, tucking back a vibrant brunette lock behind her ear.

"Alright, and for you?" the bartender continued.

"Same."

"Alright, two Classic Burgers. I'll

have that right out to you," the bartender grinned, taking up both of our menus.

Soon thereafter, Prue commented, "I'll be right back," before making her way towards the restrooms.

In Prue's absence, I nursed the cold, stout brew and watched the videos for *Imagine* by John Lennon and *Smells Like Teen Spirit* by Nirvana. Then, out of the corner of my eye, I spotted Prue. Looking over, I was struck by the simple elegance of her ensemble: glossy black heels, dark silk stockings, strapless purple dress that hugged and accentuated every curve, white gold chain draped around her neck, and a cultured pearl of deep violet in each ear. Right then, I couldn't help but feel like the luckiest man in the world.

"Hey, did you know they have Kurt Cobain's guitar back there?" Prue asked with a grin, propping herself up on the barstool.

"Yeah, last time I was here, I was sitting at the table right below it."

"Lucky."

"Have you ever been to the EMP Museum at the Seattle Center?"

"No. Wanted to go there and check it out for a while now, but still haven't made it."

"Oh my God, you would love that place! They have an entire section devoted to Nirvana: pictures, guitars, garments, even posters from when they used to play with Mudhoney."

"Seriously? That's so awesome! I used to have the biggest crush on Mark Arm," Prue commented before taking a sip of Coke.

"That's understandable. I still listen to Mudhoney."

"Me too. Have you heard their new album?"

"*Vanishing Point*? Yeah, I was down

at the Tacoma Mall a couple of weeks ago and snagged a copy at FYE."

"Oh, I love that place."

"Me too."

"So, what's your favorite song?"

"I don't remember you. No, I don't remember you," I sang in response, drawing attention from everyone else at the bar.

"How many beers have you had?" Prue chuckled, blushing from embarrassment.

"Sorry. Just the one."

"Can't take you anywhere nice," Prue scolded mockingly, wagging a finger, obviously trying to suppress her laughter.

"So, what's your favorite track?"

"Oh, it's gotta be *Douchebags on Parade*. That's some funny shit."

"Yeah, it is," I agreed

Our eyes met and the world seemed to pause for a moment.

"You really do look amazing."

"That's the second time you've commented on how I look. Have you run out of things to talk about already?"

"No, not quite. I just..."

"I know. You just can't believe you're out with a woman that's as smart, sophisticated, and sexy as me. I understand," Prue commented with a grin.

Girl's got an ego. "Well, you're not too far off. Truth be told, I had my eye on you for quite some time."

"Awe, that's sweet, but why did you wait so long to ask me out?"

"I don't know. I had my reasons I guess, but today..." I paused, glancing up at the video of *Black Hole Sun* by Soundgarden. "Today, I just felt like it was now or never."

"So, you were planning to quit?"

"Yeah, you know. After everything that happened, I just couldn't work there anymore."

"I can understand that, but the way you left..."

"I know. I shouldn't have made such a scene."

"Are you kidding me?"

"What?"

"The way you stood up to Mr. Henderson, that was great. I mean, I couldn't believe it," Prue commented with clear enthusiasm in her voice.

"Really?"

"Of course. I mean we all hate that fat, disgusting pig. He had it coming to him."

"Yeah, but..."

"But nothing. Slime-ball is always hitting on me. Rather fuck a pinecone." Leaning in, Prue continued, "Did you hear what he did at last year's Christmas party?"

"No, what?"

"He came up behind me and grabbed my ass."

"What?"

"Yeah, so I decked him."

"That was you? Was wondering who gave that bastard the black eye."

"Uh, huh. I clocked him good. Knocked him right on his ass. Thought about kicking him in the stones once I saw him down there, but decided to save that for my resignation."

"Remind me not to get on your bad side."

"Well, you don't have to worry about that. You're cute."

"What does that mean?"

"Oh, it's just that I kind of a history of letting guys walk all over me, especially the cute ones."

"Really? You don't seem like that kind of..."

"Let me ask you a question," Prue

started, cutting me off. "Have you ever cheated on anyone?"

"No, never. Never had a one-night-stand either."

"Really?"

"Yeah."

"You know, I can tell when men are lying to me."

"How's that?"

"Their lips are moving."

"No, really. I'm telling the truth."

"Sure. What makes you so special?"

"I don't know. Just have a respect for women. I think it's because I was raised by my mom."

"Oh, so you're a mama's boy."

"No," I started with a chuckle. "No, I'm definitely not a mama's boy."

"And what about a job? I mean, you did quit today."

"Yeah, so?"

"So, do you expect me to float you?"

"Huh?"

"Lookin' for a sugar mama?"

"Uh, what? No."

"'Cause if you are, you should really get with my mom. She's in full-on cougar mode. I'm sure she'd carry you along for a while, just so long you're not a bad fuck," Prue paused taking a sip of Coke. "Me, on the other hand, I can barely afford to take care of myself. Last thing I need is some guy sponging off me."

"No, I'm fine. I have some money put away and my friend Jess will let me manage the bookstore if I want."

"Jess? Is she a friend-friend, an ex-girlfriend, fuck buddy, or what?"

"Jess, Jessie, is a guy. We've been friends since elementary."

"You didn't answer my question," Prue returned, obviously trying to suppress her laughter.

"What? He has a wife and a couple

of kids."

"What's his wife's name? Bruce? Justin? Chase?"

"He's married to a woman."

"Was she born a woman?"

"Yes."

"How do you know?"

"Well, if she was born a man, the doctors did a hell of a good job."

"So, you like her?"

"Yeah, she's attractive I guess."

"Anything going on between you two?"

"What?"

"You know. Jess is at work. Kids are off at school. You just happen to be in the neighborhood."

"No. No, nothing like that."

"Does the carpet match the drapes?"

"How would I know?"

"Oh, so she goes Brazilian. Kinky."

"What? No."

"How do you know?"

"I don't."

"Yeah, that's what I thought."

"What's that supposed to mean?"

"Nothing. I'm just messing with you. You're so fun to tease," Prue said with a grin.

Just then, the bartender arrived with our entrées. "Here you go. Will there be anything else?"

"No, we're good, thanks," I replied, surveying the meal in front of me.

"Anyway, what do you have planned after dinner?" Prue continued as the bartender turned her attention to other patrons.

"Uh, well, need to go back to my apartment and…"

"Your apartment? Let me tell you something. Just 'cause you pay for a meal doesn't mean I'm open for business. What the hell kind of girl do you take me for?"

"What I was going to say, before you cut me off, is that I need to go back to my apartment and pick up some tickets I left on my dresser."

"Oh, sorry."

"It's okay."

"I'm just so used to guys that... Well, never mind. So, where are we going?"

"It's a surprise."

"Oh, I love surprises. Give me a hint?"

Chapter 5

"So, this is your apartment," Prue commented, looking around.

"Yeah, you know," I returned, closing the door.

"I was expecting something a little more..."

"Little more what?"

"I don't know. It just seems kind of bare."

"Well, I got everything I need. Beyond that, I don't give a shit."

"Well, that's good. A lot of guys I date, their place looks like a showroom –

like it came out of a magazine or
something."

"Yeah, then there are those idiots
with a man-cave. What the fuck is that?
Turn your place into a tavern?"

"I know, right?" Prue responded,
beginning to walk around. Then, spotting
my guitar, an Epiphone Special Edition
with a worn black finish and duel
humbuckers, she ran her index finger
down the fret board. "Nice guitar. You
any good?"

"Yeah, I'm pretty decent."

"Play me something?"

"Maybe later. We got to get going.
I'll get the tickets," I responded, starting
towards the bedroom.

"What do you got there?" she asked
upon my return.

I responded by handing her one of
the tickets.

"Uh, I have some bad news for you."

"What's that?"

"I've already seen this."

"But I overheard you yesterday talking to Joyce..."

"Been eavesdropping have we?" Prue asked with smile.

"Well, I just happened to overhear the conversation on my way to the restroom."

"Sure," she said with mock suspicion. "Well, you heard right. I did want to see it, but that was before my friend Lisa and I saw it last night."

"Oh."

"We can still go if you want."

"Actually, I've already seen it too."

"Then why did you buy the tickets?"

"Because... I was willing to see it again for you."

"Awe, that's so sweet," Prue started. "How 'bout that song?"

"Okay," I returned.

As I flipped on the amp and adjusted the settings, Prue positioned herself on the loveseat.

Nervously, I situated myself beside her. "Here's one you might know."

A sweet, delicate smile appeared as she moved in closer while I started to play.

"Underneath the bridge, tarp has sprung a leak. And the animals I've trapped have all become my pets. And I'm living off of grass and the drippings from the ceiling. It's okay to eat fish 'cause they don't have any feelings. Something in the way. Mmm."

"Something in the way. Mmm," Prue chimed in.

"Something in the way. Mmm," we sang in unison.

"I love that song." Prue leaned in - eyes wide, then shut.

There was a warm, soft meeting – the sweet taste of her lips, the sensation of her tongue against mine.

We touched. We caressed. And we melted into each other.

Chapter 6

The next morning was special. Waking up for the first time with someone you love, that loves you, few things can compete. Hell, nothing can compete. It's the best feeling in the world.

In the soft morning light, gazing upon Prue in slumber, I couldn't help but believe in angels; she never looked more beautiful. Feeling the warmth of her skin pressed against mine, I never felt more complete. In that moment, I was at peace. I was content. I was whole. Nothing else in the world mattered. All I wanted to do was stay there lying next to her – forever.

Eventually, Prue awoke and broke the silence, "You know what?"

"What's that?"

"My mom would absolutely love you."

"What?"

"You sure you don't want me to introduce you?" Prue asked, obviously trying to suppress her laughter.

"That's not funny."

Leave it to Prue. She was always mischievous and I loved her for it. It was part of her charm.

"Mind if I ask you a question?" she continued.

"Sure, go 'head."

"Did you ever think of me when you..."

"When I what?"

"You know."

"Why would you ask me that?"

"Just curious," Prue paused for a moment. "I thought of you."

"Really?"

"Yeah, all the time," she replied with a grin. "So, what about you?"

"Well, yeah."

"Yeah?"

"All the time."

"So, now that you've got me here, what you goin' do?" Prue asked with a playful smile.

"I'll show you," I returned, leaning in for a kiss.

♦

In the afterglow of the moment, I happened to get a glimpse of the clock-radio on my nightstand and was immediately snapped back into the world. "Oh, you're so late for work. You were supposed to be there an hour ago."

"I'm not too worried about it," Prue replied nonchalantly.

"Really?"

"Yeah, got the perfect excuse."

"What's that?"

"Female problems."

"Female problems?"

"Yeah, that's all I have to say. Works every time."

I snickered, "You're right. There's no way Stanley would call you on it and get into that conversation."

"Could you imagine if he did?"

We both broke out in laughter.

Chapter 7 ◆

God has a sense of humor. He has one fucking twisted sense of humor. There's no other way to explain it. I was right outside of Garrett's Books, literally less than five feet from the entrance, when I spotted a familiar face. It was the face of someone I was intimately acquainted with. It was the face of someone I wanted to avoid at all cost. It was the face of Phoebe Fletcher.

Phoebe was a tall, statuesque blond with piercing blue eyes, full, pouty lips, perky breasts, and legs that stretched for miles. Her wardrobe consisted almost exclusively of tight, form fitting shirts and mini-skirts – mini-skirts she wore even on the coldest of days. And, as I quickly came to find out, she usually only wore panties on "special occasions" or during her time of the month. Under most circumstances, she'd be the kind of woman that'd give a grown man wet-dreams, but there was a problem. She had an addiction. She was addicted to sex.

I met Phoebe about six months earlier. At the time, I was going through a dry spell and was getting to the point where I'd fuck anything that moved. I even started eying my 84-year-old neighbor, Mrs. Gruber. Wondered how far I could shove that cane up her ass. I wondered what it would be like to get a blowjob from someone with no teeth. That's when I started to scare myself.

That's when I decided to do something drastic. That's when I decided to go to Chaste – a support group for those suffering from sexual addiction.

I don't know where I first heard about Chaste. To be honest, I wasn't even sure if such a group existed, but I went online and sure enough. There was a meeting the following day at St. James Cathedral and I decided to attend.

Going in, I was pretty nervous. Hell, I was petrified. Still, for some reason, I proceeded. I knew what I was doing was wrong. I knew that the group was for people suffering from a compulsion. I knew the group was for people in need, but I didn't care. I needed to get laid.

The chapter was run by retired Psychologist Dr. Martin Prig; everyone called him Dr. Marty.

To tell you the truth, I didn't really care for the guy. He tried to come off as supportive and mild mannered, but it was obviously an act. Instead, he was a self-righteous control freak. And new-comers had to address the group; he insisted.

I sat there in that cold basement, in that awkwardly uncomfortable folding chair, in that circle facing all the others. I sat there with questions swirling in my head. Was I the only liar? Was I the only one so weak and pathetic to be that damned depraved? Did they know?

I sat there, listening to story after story. Some of them, most of them, broke down in tears: bloodshot eyes, sniveling, tightly grasped wads of used Kleenex. Most of them broke down, but not Phoebe. Phoebe was unapologetic. Phoebe was a predator.

It seems Phoebe had been recently dismissed from her job as a flight attendant with Alaska Airlines. During a flight from Portland to SeaTac, a passenger, a nun of all people – Sister Mary Sebastian, went to use the lavatory and found Phoebe in the middle of a ménage à toris with two young black guys. Come to find out, they both played basketball for Seattle University. How they all fit into the lavatory of a 737, I'll never know.

Up next was one sick bastard. His name was Steve Buscemi and I swear he looked just like the actor, but I'm sure it wasn't really him. For one thing, this guy was noticeably younger. He also spoke with a thick Southern drawl. Anyway, he was arrested for indecent exposure and animal cruelty after neighbors reported that he was fucking his German Shepherd, Roxi, on the front lawn. "The bitch was in heat, so I fucked her. What's wrong with that?"

It was my turn next. I didn't know what to say, so I said whatever popped in my head. "Hi, my name is Adrian." There was no way in hell I was going to give my real name.

"Hi Adrian," the group responded in unison.

"Hey. Well, I was let go yesterday from my job because my secretary, my fuckin' secretary off all people, turned me in for sexual harassment."

"What happened?" Dr. Marty inquired, with mock sympathy, after a moment of silence.

"Okay, so I texted her a pic of my dick with the message, 'Ready for your raise?' So what? Who the hell doesn't hit on their secretary, huh?" What a load of bullshit. I've never done anything even remotely close to that, but they bought it. They all bought it.

For the remainder of the session, all I could think about was who I'd proposition when it was all over. There was Caroline – a cute, robust redhead with an affinity for bikers. She was my first choice 'til she caught me eyeing her long, sumptuous legs and flashed me a look to kill. Samantha, a feisty little brunette, caught my attention until I found out she was a prostitute. I have enough problems; last thing I need is VD. An adorable blond named Natalie really had me going: beautiful blue eyes, gorgeous figure, smile that'd light up a room. Still, she was a mom and I just couldn't do that. It didn't seem right. Of course, there was Phoebe, but she just seemed out of my league. So, all-in-all, it appeared as if my dry-spell would continue indefinitely.

After the meeting, I made a beeline to the restroom. Maybe it was the Nachos Bell Grande catching up with me. Maybe it was just nerves, but I needed to take a shit.

Afterwards, when I opened the door

of the stall, there was a surprise waiting for me. Phoebe was propped up on the counter with her skirt pulled up. She must have been horny as hell, because she wasn't even deterred from the lingering stench of my deposit. "See anything you like?"

I couldn't help but become intoxicated by the wild look in her eyes. I couldn't help but eye her amber landing strip. I couldn't help but notice the ring in her clit. I couldn't help but take her right then and there.

Following our escapades in the restroom, we went back to her place. Neither one of us got any sleep.

The next day, I had mixed feelings about Phoebe. Sure, she had the body of a goddess. Sure, she had experience and did things I'd never even dreamed of before. Sure, I was glad my dry spell was over, but she was insensible. My balls ached. My balls ached so bad I could hardly concentrate on work. Hell, I could hardly walk. Still, I kept seeing her – for a couple of weeks anyhow. Finally, after much deliberation, I decided to avoid her; she was just too much for me. The pain won out over the pleasure.

In the days that ensued after my decision, she called a couple of times, but that was it. I hadn't seen or heard from her since. That is, not until that day outside of Garrett's Books.

"Adrian!" Phoebe yelled, starting to run towards me.

Oh shit. "Hey."

"Hey, you son-of-a-bitch! Stand me up! Can't answer your fuckin' phone? I thought we had a good time together, then you up and vanish? What the fuck is wrong with you?!"

"I'm sorry. I was just going through a weird period in my life."

"Yeah, whatever. That's no excuse."

"Well..."

"What the fuck are you doing here anyhow? Track me down? Wanna fuck me again, is that it?" Phoebe interrupted.

"No, I'm here to see about a job."

"What?"

"Yeah, the owner Jess is an old friend. We've known each other since elementary."

"You're Shane?"

"Yeah."

"We were together for three fuckin' weeks and you didn't even tell me your real name?"

"Well, I was embarrassed. You know, I went to that meeting when I really shouldn't have. I'm not..."

"I told you things..." she stammered, cutting me off.

"I know. I'm sorry."

"If you tell him anything, anything

at all, I'll cut your fuckin' dick off!"

"Whoa, whoa, whoa. Why the fuck would you care if I told Jess anything about you, huh? He's married with kids."

"Because I work here, you fuckin' asshole."

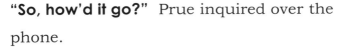

Chapter 8

"So, how'd it go?" Prue inquired over the phone.

"Well, you're talking to the new manager of Garrett's Books."

"Oh, that's wonderful. Congratulations."

"Thank you, it's just..."

"Just what?"

"One of the employees, Phoebe..."

"Yeah?"

"Well, we have kind of a history."

"You still like her?" Prue asked with a hint of insecurity in her voice.

"God no. No, not at all."

"Oh, then she still likes you?"

"No, she can't stand me. I mean, she absolutely hates my guts."

"What happened between you two?"

"Well, we met at Chaste and..."

"Chaste? Isn't that the support group for sexual addiction?"

"Yeah... Uh, long story."

"Sounds like it."

"I'll tell you about it later."

"Okay."

There was a short, awkward pause between us. Then, Prue continued, "So, you at the bookstore now?"

"No, I don't start 'til tomorrow. I'm actually up at the Seattle Center; walking by the Space Needle right now headed towards the Armory."

"Oh, we can meet for lunch. Have you eaten yet?" Prue asked with a faint hint of excitement in her voice.

"No, that sounds good. You want to eat at Sky City?"

"Actually, I just meant meeting at the Armory. I really love that Bigfoot Barbeque place. Besides, I don't really think I have time to eat at the Space Needle right now: have to get the tickets, wait in line for the elevator, then the restaurant is usually packed. Even if we just ate at the café on the observation deck..."

"Yeah, you're right. Besides, the view is much better at night."

"Exactly. It'd be better to just do that some weekend; have a nice romantic dinner."

"It's a deal."

"I'm goin' to hold you to it," Prue responded with a chuckle.

"So, meet you at the Armory in ten minutes?"

"Sounds great."

Chapter 9

A period of new love is life at its most
provocative state. It's when a thousand
moments create a thousand memories and
someone hardly known before becomes
familiar, becomes necessity, and becomes
imprinted on your very soul. After which,
you never dream of being apart. You
never felt more alive and wonder as to how
you ever got along without them. They
become the sun in your hair, wind at your
back, air in your lungs, and blood in your
veins. All of this, all of it, happens so fast
– in the blink of an eye. The mind races to

record it all, but fails. So, what you're left with is a thousand images, stories, and fragments from a thousand different moments.

Looking back on the time Prue and I shared, I'm absolutely overwhelmed by the myriad of experiences we shared.

Of course, I remember that evening. It was the first time I ever been to her place. And her place was the last thing I expected. She lived on a boat docked at the Nickerson Marina – The Merlot.

The story goes that her grandfather, Harold Baker, built the vessel shortly after returning home from his tour of duty in Europe and the Pacific during the Second World War. Although Harold originally intended to sail around the West Coast and perhaps up to Alaska with his new bride, Selma, those plans were put on hold when she became pregnant with Prue's father, Christopher – Chris for short.

Weeks later, Harold died suddenly of heart-failure.

Since that time, the Merlot has been rarely used and the engine has gone into disrepair; however, the vessel still has a functional electrical system and plumbing.

Following Prue through the gate and down to the long walkway lined with storage containers and the covered docks, I didn't know what to expect. It was a pleasant surprise to find a seemingly well-kept vessel docked in 13.

After entering through the back part of the boat, we passed through the bedroom and entered a spacious living space complete with a couch and full entertainment center.

"What do you think?" Prue inquired, watching for my reaction.

Nearly overwhelmed with the aroma of marinara, pasta, and spices, I replied, "It's nice." It was then I noticed a small galley kitchen and a built-in dining table at the bottom of a small flight of stairs near the bow.

"Glad you like it. Why don't you have a seat and I'll dish us up?" Prue said, motioning towards the sofa before making her way down to the galley.

It would prove to be an evening to remember. We ate spaghetti with Italian sausage and garlic toast. We shared a bottle of Beringer Merlot. We split a generous slice of cherry cheesecake – letting each mouthful melt, savoring every morsel. We watched old *Twilight Zone* episodes on Netflix well into the night. We made love accompanied by the gentle motion of the rolling waves. We fell asleep in each other's arms.

Chapter 10 ◆

I think it was that next weekend, we went to the Seattle Aquarium and hung-out on the Waterfront.

"Oh my God! That's so cute!" Prue squealed, looking at the River Otter.

The otter was quite adorable – asleep next to the glass, facing out.

It was the perfect photo op and Prue didn't hesitate to digitally capture the moment with an iPhone camera app.

I came up from behind and took Prue by the waist and there we stood. There we stood, watching the otter in silence. There we stood, in the moment. There we stood, until Prue finally broke the silence.

"Where to now?"

"Think we've seen everything. You hungry?"

"Yeah, I could eat. What were you thinking?"

"Ivar's?"

"Sounds good," Prue returned with a slight chuckle, obviously a response to the subtle irony of leaving an aquarium to go have fish and chips.

And there we went. We both had a four piece. Shared an order of coleslaw. And I was sure to save some fries for the seagulls.

"You better watch it or you'll lose a finger," Prue cautioned as I approached a gull perched on a railing post with my basket of fries.

"No worries. The trick is to pinch

the very tip of the fry and hold it out," I responded while demonstrating.

In a flash, the gull snatched the fry in its beak and swallowed it whole.

"Oh my God!"

I held out another.

Gone.

"That's awesome," Prue grinned.

Chapter 11

"**I haven't been to a Mariners game** in years. And last time I went, it was at the Kingdome," Prue confessed.

"Mean you still haven't been to Safeco Field?"

"No, been over here at Century Link though," motioning her head. "Saw the Sounders play a little while back and went to a Seahawks game last year."

"That's awesome!"

"I know, right?"

Spotting a Jones vender behind their corporate headquarters, I asked,

"Want anything?"

"Cream soda."

"Two cream sodas," I relayed to the vender – a guy with closely cropped brown hair, dressed in jeans and a Jones Soda tee.

"That'll be two dollars," he responded.

I handed him the money and he retracted two cans of cream soda from the barrel-shaped cooler.

As he passed a can each to Prue and me, I commented, "Don't see Jones in a can very often."

"Nah. You just be sure to recycle, alright?"

"Will do."

Continuing down the street between Century Link and a row of mostly sports apparel shops, which was peppered with various vendors taking advantage of the game day crowd, a guy approached me,

"What's up? You mad bro?"

"What are you talkin' about?"

"Saw the way you looked at me, man. You got a problem?"

"As a matter of fact, I do. Couldn't help but notice your Cubs jersey."

"And what about it, man? Love me some Cubbies. They're my team!"

"Yeah, it's idiots like you that cost us the Sonics."

"Don't lay that trip on me, man," he responded before taking a long drag off a smoldering joint.

"All I'm saying is you need to support the home team. Support the home team!"

"Ah, you're totally right, man," He paused, taking a short puff. "Gotta find me some grub."

"What was that all about?" Prue asked as the Cubs fan wandered off.

"I have no idea."

Chapter 12

"Why is it I'm up here smelling tobacco when weed's been legalized?" Mudhoney frontman Mark Arm asked the crowd.

To celebrate their 25th Anniversary, the influential Indie label Sub Pop hosted the Silver Jubilee: a free concert on three stages in Seattle's historic Georgetown neighborhood.

To be honest, I was surprised Soundgarden didn't make an appearance. And the surviving members of Nirvana were nowhere to be found. Still, it was an awesome experience. Getting to see

Mudhoney was just the cherry on top.

"Doesn't look like he's aged a bit," I commented to Prue, shouting over the crowd and the ringing in my ears.

"I know, right?" she responded with a grin. "Want some earplugs?"

"What?"

"Want some earplugs?"

I should have worn earplugs, but it completely slipped my mind. Still, it seemed as if it didn't matter. All day, with the countless other bands Prue and I listened to, my hearing remained fully intact. It wasn't until Mudhoney took the stage that everything became muffled. Still, I didn't really care. If I went deaf, at least the last thing I got to hear was Mudhoney and that was alright with me.

"No, afraid it's too late for that," I responded.

"I told you so." Prue didn't say it — not verbally anyhow, but I could see it in her eyes. Moreover, she didn't seem angry or even mildly irritated, but concerned. That too was clearly in her eyes. She worried for me. She cared for me. And I knew she loved me.

As the next song began to thunder from the cluster of amps, the crowd exploded. Teens cut through the crowd and made their way towards the stage for their shot at surfing the crowd.

"Douchebags on parade!" Prue and I screamed in unison along with Arm.

Chapter 13

They say that the spice of life is variety.
And, for the most part, I agree; however, it
is also quite important to stick with what
works. Contradictory as this may seem, it
is completely true. The key is simply
moderation. For example, in a
relationship, it is important to go out,
have fun, and be open to new experiences.
Although, that does not mean a couple
should venture outside of the relationship.
In fact, quite the opposite. A couple
should be a partnership that compliments
both individuals. A couple should come to

rely on each other. A couple should be stronger together than they could ever be apart.

Prue and I were such a couple.

◆

It was a day quite unlike the widely held, and typically true, stereotype of Western Washington weather. Instead, it was warm with only lightly scattered clouds. In the distance, Mt. Rainier was fully visible and somehow seemed closer than ever. And that's where we decided to go.

When heading to Rainier, there are several destinations to choose from – all of them beautiful, all of them serene; however, none compare to Sunrise.

At 6,400 feet, Sunrise is the highest point that be reached by vehicle and offers breathtaking views of the summit as well as the sprawling Cascade Range.

We arrived just before noon and

found a shaded picnic table nestled in an outcropping of pines.

"What'd you bring?" Prue asked anxiously as I sat the cooler on the table.

"Well, I made some turkey wraps..." I started, unpacking the cooler.

"Are those the things with cream-cheese and jalapeno slices?"

"Yeah."

"Oh, I love those."

I grinned and continued, "Got some potato wedges. Some carrots and celery with ranch. Got that smoked peperoni we picked up at Stewart's Meats. And..."

"Yeah?"

"Brought some of those little bottles of Chardonnay you like," I replied before handing her a bottle.

"You know, you'll make a good wife someday," Prue responded with a playful grin, obviously trying to suppress her laughter.

I tried to shake my head in disapproval, but I couldn't help but smile. I loved her playful mischievousness.

"So good. Thank you," Prue commented after taking a bite from a turkey wrap.

Ask her. "No problem... Uh, there was something I wanted to talk to you about."

"Oh, no. This can't be good."

"No, it's just we've been spending so much time together and you're always staying over. Have your own drawer..."

"Is this the I-need-some-space routine? Is that what this is? Think I'm suffocating you? 'Cause let me tell you, I've seen this kinda shit from a lot of guys, but I didn't expect it from you. Not from you," Prue interjected with an unsteady voice, clearly full of hurt, as a tear coursed down her cheek.

"No. No. That's not it at all.

Actually, quite the opposite. I want you to move in with me."

"What?"

Our eyes locked.

All at once, I was overcome by the beauty and warmth that resided in those deep hazel pools. All at once, I was drawn in. All at once, I was complete.

"I want you to move in with me."

"Really?"

"Really."

At that moment, I could tell something changed. The fear and the hurt Prue carried from a lifetime of loves and lovers lost suddenly melted away. The hesitation and expectations of rejection were gone. She was free. I could see it so clearly in her eyes. Prue was free.

Chapter 14 ◆

It was a particularly hard day at the bookstore. James Mayhugh, the next big thing in the publishing world, stopped by on his book tour to promote his latest novel, *The Revengers*.

Before he arrived, I was expecting to meet a pale, pasty-faced shut-in wearing well-worn, casual clothing with medium-length partially-tangled hair, three days growth, and thick black-framed glasses. I also thought he'd be kind of shy and awkward. It's just what I envisioned after meeting so many other authors. The man

I met, however, was nothing of the kind. Instead, he looked like he belonged in a cubical at Emerald International. He had well-groomed, closely-cropped hair, was clean-shaven, and wore a white button-down shirt with black slacks and leather loafers. Surprisingly, he also seemed quite personable – insisted I call him James. The only thing I got right were his glasses.

Anyway, the place was packed. People came from all over to meet James and get a signed copy of his book. Some bought two, three copies. At one point, the line stretched out the door and down the block.

Behind the counter, it was just me and Chris Lowery.

Chris was an English major at the University of Washington and worked part-time. Come to find out, he actually started at the Tacoma campus and lived in an apartment with his girlfriend – Linda or Lydia or something like that. I don't remember. Anyway, they were together for about three-years and were beginning to talk about marriage when it all started to fall apart.

Memorial Day weekend, they decided to go out to Spanaway and visit his folks. And, of course, they brought their dog with them – a Miniature Husky named Rascal. Well, almost as soon as they arrived, Chris' dad got all indigent and talked about how he didn't want the dog in the house: it sheds, it shits, it slobbers. So, they compromised and agreed to have Rascal stay in the pet-carrier at all times when he was in the house. Okay fine, right?

Well, that night Chris went to feed the dog and didn't latch the carrier completely. A couple of minutes later, Chris' girlfriend walked in the guestroom and found Rascal had taken a dump on the floor. So, she went to the kitchen to get some paper-towels. Meanwhile, Chris' dad wondered what was going on, walked in the guestroom, and went completely ballistic.

Long story short, Chris' girlfriend grabbed Rascal and ran out to the car. Chris came out of the bathroom with no idea what was going on and his parents screaming at him. He barely made it out to the car before Linda or Lydia, or whatever the hell her name is, sped off.

The whole way home, Chris' girlfriend was in tears. And, of course, she blamed Chris for the whole thing. After that, things just went downhill.

Anyhow, it was just me and Chris working the registers and we were completely swamped. I mean it was crazy.

Then, two minutes before her shift was supposed to start, Phoebe called in sick – no surprise there. I'm sure she was just trying to screw with me.

Jess had his hands full attending to customers. Every now and then, I'd see him darting here and there with people in-tow or carrying stacks of books.

Yeah, it was a regular three-ring-circus, but I didn't mind. Jess needed all the business he could get. Ever since eReaders and tablets started popping up everywhere, the store has been in a gradual decline. Book signings, however, always brought in a lot of money – especially with authors like James Mayhugh. The reason is really quite simple. The experience of meeting an author in-person, sharing a bit of dialogue, and getting a signed memento of the occasion is something unique – something special. It's something technology can't ever duplicate.

Finally, James was on his way, the

lines subsided, and a sense of normalcy returned. In the afterglow, I remember thinking it was like the changing of some great tide – from chaos to tranquility.

I offered to stay and help Jess count down the drawers, tally the safe, and make the deposit, but he insisted that I go home and relax; that's just the kind of stand-up guy he is. So, I took my signed copies of *The Revengers* (one for me, one for Prue, and three that would show up on Christmas morning in the hands of those I had no idea what to get) and headed out.

After an extraordinarily grueling day, I was looking forward to returning to at least some modicum of a routine: having a pleasant meal with Prue, talking about our days, curling up together on the sofa and watching some mindless sitcom, retiring to the bedroom and maybe having some mid-week sex – nothing too kinky or protracted, but satisfying. When Prue opened the door, however, I knew it was going to be a night unlike any other.

Chapter 15 ◆

The door opened to Prue standing in the doorway. She didn't say a word. On her face was a mixed expression of what seemed like joy and concern.

Swollen red eyes and smeared mascara told the story of her tears.

"What's wrong? What is it?"

She responded by holding up a small, slender object and, all at once, I knew what it was.

Oh my God. "You're...?"

She nodded yes as small, fragile grin began to emerge.

"You're pregnant?"

"Yes," she whispered with a smile.

In a single motion, I dropped the bag of books and took her up in my arms.

We kissed. We kissed with an explosive passion – a blissful, pure expression of our love. It was a celebration of circumstance and a symbol of all we could ever hope to be.

In that moment, I knew the answer to the question that had plagued me. I knew the time was finally at hand.

Gently, I sat Prue down on the sofa, got down on one knee, retrieved the ring-box from my jacket pocket and, with her warm hazel eyes in mine, asked the only question that still matters in this damn world, "Will you marry me?"

Death

View from Mt. Pleasant Cemetery, Seattle, WA

"The lives we make never seem to get us anywhere but dead."

Soundgarden
The Day I Tried to Live

Chapter 16

She was dead. Prue was dead.

Just eighteen hours after Prue gave me the news, eighteen hours since I popped the question, eighteen hours after she said "yes," I received the call from Lt. Randy Disher of the Seattle Police Department. Prue was dead.

At first, the details were sketchy, but after a day or so of talking with police and former co-workers at Emerald International, I was able to piece together the whole story. It seems Julia McDougal, Stanley Henderson's latest in a long line of personal secretaries, had called in sick – probably to interview somewhere else. So Stanley, being the lazy bastard that he is, told Prue to go pick-up his dry-cleaning.

A couple of blocks away, while headed up Spring, Prue inexplicitly had a blowout of the right-front tire and was sent careening onto Fourth headed the wrong way. Quickly, she swerved to avoid a Toyota Tacoma pulling out from Safeco Plaza which inadvertently set her in the path of the 545 Sound Transit line headed in from Tacoma. As a result, Prue attempted to take refuge on the plaza in front of the Central Library, but didn't quite make it.

The bus collided with her at about a forty-five degree angle – sending Prue into the driver's side window with enough force to fracture her skull.

When paramedics found Prue at the scene, she was unconscious and barely breathing. She would later be pronounced DOA at Harborview Medical Center.

Later, when I went to see the scene for myself, I found the remnants of a shattered Jones Soda bottle some reckless asshole must have thrown out onto the street. I believe it triggered the accident. Ironically, it was a bottle of Orange and Cream – my favorite.

Shortly after the accident, after Prue was DOA at Harborview, the police went through her contact list. That's where they found me – listed as "Future Hubby."

I agreed to identify the body.

It was her.

Afterwards, I walked around. I walked around aimlessly in the rain for hours – cold, wet, numb.

I walked to Westlake Center.

I rode the monorail to the Seattle Center.

I rode the elevator to the top of the

Space Needle.

I wandered past the occupied café tables and tourists, of every description, lined up at the kiosks waiting to email friends and loved ones their complimentary souvenir photo.

I walked down the steps and out onto the observation deck.

I walked to the railing and climbed up.

I looked out over the city and felt the cool wind on my face.

I thought about jumping.

I wanted to jump, but I didn't.

I was a coward.

Chapter 17

Wish I could give you a detailed account of what happened next, in the days following Prue's death, but I can't. I can't because I was in a fog, in a daze, and everything just went by so fast. Instead, all that remain are fragments and shards, but I'll tell you what I remember.

I remember visiting the scene of the accident and finding the remains of the soda bottle. There I was, walking down the sidewalk on Fourth in the same direction Prue had traveled, when I noticed sunlight glinting off something in the street.

Normally, I would have ignored such a thing. Normally, I would have just kept walking; however, for some reason on that particular day, I was intrigued.

Lying shattered on the wet asphalt were the remains of the bottle. Despite the rain and traffic, the label was still clearly legible. The innocent face of a young girl, captured in black and white, stared back at me.

All at once, I suspected, I knew the significance of the bottle. All at once, I was captivated by it.

Finally, I was snapped back to reality by the blaring of a horn.

"Hey, move it, asshole!" a thin, wiry man with dark, slicked back hair and tobacco stained teeth yelled from the window of his bright red Honda Civic.

In response, I hurriedly seized the neck of the bottle (which remained largely in-tact) by the cap and retreated to the sidewalk.

Days later, I placed the bottle fragment in its new home on the corner of my nightstand. By that time, thanks to Things Remembered, it was centered in a clear acrylic case. At the very bottom, an elongated oval of polished silver was engraved with the words "never forget."

♦

Prue must have known we were meant for each other well before I proposed. I know this because, much to my surprise, she had put her life insurance in my name.

The policy she had through Emerald International was for fifty-thousand dollars. Since her death was deemed work related, however, the insurance company paid double. Three days after Prue's death, I received a check for one-hundred thousand dollars.

To be honest, the money didn't make any difference. All the money in the world wouldn't have been any consolation. Instead, I felt awkward, dirty. Even though Prue's death was in no way my fault, I felt as though I'd done something terribly wrong. I felt as though I was somehow profiting from Prue's death. And it just made me hate myself that much more.

♦

Over and over again, I asked myself the same questions. Night after night, I'd lay awake. Throughout the day, no matter what I was doing, the questions would seep back into my consciousness. *Why did it have to be her? Why would God take someone so beautiful – so perfect? Why couldn't He take an asshole like me instead? Why? Why? Why does He hate me so fucking much?! Why did He have to take the only thing in my life that was worth living for? Why am I still here?!*

◆

I remember sitting with a bowl of Orange Chicken with steamed rice in front of me, surrounded by former co-workers.

For the first time, I was the center-of-attention. I was an anomaly in their mundane world and they gathered around like moths to a flame.

They offered their condolences. More than lip-service, I could tell they were sincere – or at least wanted to be: eyes weighed with sadness, tragedy on their lips.

They offered what they knew.

Someone else was drawn to the scene and made their way through the crowd – someone that wanted more than anything to be the center-of-attention. It was none other than Stanley Henderson.

He met me eye-to-eye across the table and it was clear he offered no apology. There was no sorrow in his way. There was no remorse in his face. Instead, there was only distain.

Before he could utter a single word, I pounced across the table, landed my hands around his throat, and took him to the ground – all in a single, fluid motion.

Immediately, his face turned a glowing beet red. His eyes bulged.

Stanley tried to speak, to call for help, but was only able to produce a loud gurgling sound.

Stanley tried to worm his way out from beneath me, but I had him pinned.

Stanley tried to pull my hands from his throat, but only displayed his own impotence.

"Come along, sucka."

Ross Jefferson to the rescue. Standing at 6'-5", the guy was all muscle and carried his self like a Spartan going into battle. Really, he looked more like a lineman for the Seahawks rather than a security officer.

We never really had occasion to talk. Actually, truth be told, I usually tried to avoid him. Still, I heard through the rumor mill that he was a pretty decent guy – wife, and kids, and all that. I also heard that he was originally from Detroit, Michigan, but moved to Everett as a kid to live with an aunt and uncle. Apparently, his parents died in auto accident just weeks before Christmas when he was only six. Also, it seems after high school, he earned a full-ride scholarship to play for the U-Dub, but was kicked out of the program after a drug test found steroids in his system.

Anyway, both of my arms were arrested in a vice-like grip before I was pulled off of Stanley and tossed aside.

"I'll give yo' ass to the count of ten to get the hell up outta here! One..."

And with that, I was gone.

Looking back on it now, I'm disturbed by my behavior. Not because of my actions, but because I wasn't in control. I never made a conscious decision to kill Stanley, but there I was, on the ground strangling the life out of him. That look in his eyes set me off and I could have killed him. I would have killed him if Ross hadn't shown up.

What disturbs me more is the not knowing. What will set me off in the future? What if no one is there to stop me? What if I kill someone without one single solitary thought?

Temporary insanity. Experts call it temporary insanity. What it really is, however, is a momentary relapse. It is a fleeting period in which the modern restraints of civilization are cast aside and one acts on the instincts that carried us through thousands of years of evolution.

It is a moment in which one is truly wild.

Buried deep down in every one of us is something wild – something uncontrollable. No matter how civilized we pretend to be, it's always there just below the surface.

We are animals.

♦

Of course, no matter how hard I try to forget, I still remember making the funeral arrangements. What I remember most is the showroom – the casket showroom. Spread out across the dull white room was an array of caskets of all different sizes and colors. Most looked like pills to be swallowed by the Earth, but a few really stood out. One, a child-sized coffin, was made to look like the Teenage Mutant Ninja Turtles' van.

Because of her stature, Prue would fit in a child-sized coffin, but I really had no desire to send my fiancée off in a mini anything. She deserved the absolute best and I could afford it. Anything less would just be plain disrespectful.

Looking around, I quickly realized that choosing a coffin wasn't as simple as it would seem. There were different materials, different gages, and different designs. And I did have one question.

"Why are they padded?"

"Excuse me, sir?" Mortimer Reynolds, the salesman of sorts, replied politely. Still, I could tell he was a bit annoyed with the question.

"What's with all the cushion and padding? And the pillows. What's with the pillows? I mean, they're dead. It's a little too late to worry about comfort."

"Sir, you're right of course. It would be positively absurd to worry about the comfort of the dead; however, the padding and such is merely for appearances. It's meant to comfort friends and loved ones by giving the impression the departed have slipped into an eternal slumber. It's meant to look as though they are resting peacefully."

"Well, if that's the case, why aren't people buried in their pajamas?"

"Sir?"

"I know. I'm just... Sorry."

To tell the truth, at that moment, I felt like a horse's ass. I knew it was a serious occasion. I knew that Prue's family, friends, and co-workers were all counting on me to arrange a proper memorial. I knew that it was the last thing on Earth I could ever do for Prue and our unborn child. Still, there I was. Thankfully, Mortimer replied with an explanation I could take some solace in.

"That's quite alright, sir. I've been doing this job for twenty-two years and I've seen it all. There are those who are obviously distraught, but are able to muddle through the process of making arrangements in a fairly straight-forward manner. Others can't go two minutes without breaking down in tears. Then there are those, like yourself, that can't really cope, so they detach themselves from the situation – usually through humor. It's all perfectly normal. Everyone grieves in their own way."

I felt a bit insulted. Not by what he said, mind you, but by how effortlessly he was able to categorize me and put me in a box – so to speak.

"So, have you reached a decision?" Mortimer continued after a couple of moments.

"Yes, this one over here. The cream with pink lining."

"Excellent choice."

Chapter 18 ♦

Standing graveside at Mt. Pleasant Cemetery, after it was all said and done and the crowd of mourners in shades of black slipped back into the gray misty haze, I was transported to a moment not a month past. Prue and I were aboard a ferry, the Walla Walla, between Bremerton and Seattle. At first we sat side-by-side as usual, just inside the seating area near what was the bow on that particular trip. We sat, both reading from a Kindle.

If memory serves me, I was reading... Well, who gives a fuck what I was reading? I'm sure you don't. The point is, I got so involved in the story that I didn't notice when Prue had gotten up. When I finally did look up, I was startled to not see her there.

It wasn't that I expected her to be by my side every moment like she was on a leash or something. Fact is, I liked that she was a strong, independent woman with her own thoughts and opinions. Her willingness to say and do as she damn well pleased is one of the things that attracted me to her. Still, staring there at the empty seat, I was overcome with a sense of loss. Maybe even panic.

Of course, these feelings were irrational. She couldn't get very far on a ferry in the Sound. Looking back on it now, I think I reacted that way because I had so many relationships come and go over the years. I had my share of heartbreak and was afraid I'd lose Prue too.

Then I spotted her out at the railing facing the wind – hair waving. She looked so calm, so serene, so beautiful.

At that moment, I appreciated just how lucky I was. And I knew, without a doubt, that I wanted to spend the rest of my life with her.

At that moment, standing graveside, I never felt more alone.

I watched drop-after-drop impact, pool, and cascade down the glossy cream finish.

I watched the well-manicured blades of grass ruffle with each gust.

I released and watched a single red rose drift down and settle dead center.

"I love you, Prudence."

Chapter 19

A week after the funeral, I was spending a day off parked on the sofa in my boxers playing a monster session of *Resident Evil 4* on the Wii when my cell rang.

"Hello?"

"Hey, it's Alex – Prue's brother. We met at the funeral."

"Oh yeah, hey. What's going on?"

"Uh well, here's the thing. I was a couple of months behind on my rent and umm..."

"You need to borrow some money?" I asked, cutting him off.

"Oh no. No. I, uh, came back to my apartment and there was an eviction notice on my door."

"That sucks."

"Yeah, tell me about it."

There was a brief, awkward pause.

I knew what he wanted. Still, I was going to make him say it.

"Well anyway, I was wondering if I could crash at your place for a little while. You know, until I get back on my feet."

"Uh, well..."

"You know, I wouldn't ask, but you are kinda like family."

"What about your folks?"

"My parents? Are you kidding? Last time I stayed with them, they gave me a ten o' clock curfew and they wouldn't let me bring any ladies to the house."

"Well..."

"Come on, man. Do me a solid and I'll totally owe you one. Alright?"

"Okay, fine. But only for a little while."

"Alright. Thank you, man. You won't regret it. I swear."

"No problem." *What the hell did I just agree to?*

Chapter 20

I'm sure you remember what happened next, or at least I hope you do. We spoke about it at length. Prue's bother, Alexander Baker (Alex), moved in with me.

Despite what you might think, Alex was a great guy: outgoing, friendly, and always ready with a joke. The man was hilarious – absolutely hilarious. And the thing of it is, I really enjoyed his company. Here I was, this natural born introvert, and he was the life-of-the-party. He was everything I wanted to be: carefree, spontaneous, full-of-life. Unfortunately, that was only half the story.

Two-weeks, almost two-weeks to the day after Alex started staying on my sofa, I got a rude awakening.

"What the fuck?!"

"Huh?" Alex mumbled.

"What the fuck is this?"

That day, I just happened to forget my wallet at the apartment, so I went back during lunch to pick it up. That's when I found Alex propped up on the sofa – his arm tied-off with one of my ties. Not just any tie, mind you, but my expensive crimson silk tie that I got compliments on every time I wore it – my power tie. And lying on the carpet was a needle – a needle I nearly stepped on when I rushed over to Alex.

Suddenly, with truth right in my face, I felt like such a fool. There were all those signs. There were all those warning signs and I just didn't see it   .

Alex slurred his speech from time-to-time, but I thought he was just drunk.

Alex was always fidgety, but I thought that was just his way – maybe suffered from a nervous condition.

Alex always wore long sleeves, but who the hell was I to give fashion advice?

Alex didn't seem to particularly care about his appearance and was always grungy, but that's not too out-of-the-ordinary in Seattle.

Once, on the coffee table, I found a spoon with the bottom all covered in soot, but I still couldn't put two and two together.

Under normal circumstances, I know I would have recognized what was going on right under my nose, but those weren't normal circumstances. I was living in a fog.

Yes, I know I should have thrown him out right then and there. And, to be honest, there was a part of me that wanted to – that really wanted to, but I just couldn't do it. He was, after all, Prue's brother. Still, after that, the pretense was over. Alex no longer tried to hide his addiction. The great guy, the life-of-the-party, was gone. In his places was an irritable, bruiting, self-loathing individual that hated the world and everyone in it – especially me.

Of course, you know how I reacted. Still mourning the death of my pregnant fiancée, there was no way I could deal with Alex and what he'd become. There was no way I could try and get him the help he needed when it took everything I had just to get out of bed in the morning.

I wanted to die. I wanted to die and still do. It's really all I think about anymore. Not just the whether or not, but the how. I wonder if the Church is right. Is there really a hell besides the one I'm

living? No. I tell myself I don't believe. I
tell myself that organized religion is simply
a crutch for the feeble-minded. I tell
myself that "faith" is nothing more than a
license to be blissfully ignorant – an
excuse to be apathetic to the world around
us. I tell myself that the only consequence
of suicide is a sweet and lasting release. I
tell myself these things, yet still I wonder.
Could I be wrong? Is this what I actually
believe, or is it simply what I want to
believe? I don't know.

For the time being, thanks to you, I
have a purpose. Still, when I'm done and
my story's out there, I think I'll be free to
leave.

Anyway, less than a week after my
discovery, I started shooting-up as well.

At first, I admit, I was just curious.
After a single hit though, I was hooked. It
alleviated the tension. It absolved the
fears. It clouded the memories. It eased

the pain. And when they all resurfaced, salvation was only a syringe away.

The next couple of months are mostly a blur. In fact, the next thing I really remember is waking up at the Swedish Medical Center: clear tubing, wires, the thin gown, antiseptic, KOMO news broadcast, rhythmic beeping, a dull mechanical drone as you adjusted your bed, pitter-patter of rain on the window, the cool pillow, crisp sheets, thick metal guardrails, the catheter. I remember the catheter well.

It seems, earlier that day, Phoebe found me in the stockroom of Garrett's Books sprawled out on the floor unconscious and barely breathing. As a credit to her, despite our past, she called the paramedics. According to what the attending physician, Dr. Swanson, would later tell me, I had a potentially lethal overdose. Actually, I'd been clinically dead

for almost a minute and they had to
resuscitate me.

Chapter 21 ♦

"Hey. I'm Alan Welker, and you are?" you asked, in a surprisingly friendly tone, propped up on your elbow.

Honestly, I was initially annoyed that you were attempted to start a conversation. Fact is, I wasn't feeling all that well and rather you'd just keep to yourself. My own personal hell of withdraw had begun: nausea, headache, stomach cramps. It took everything I had not to blow chunks and it'd only get worse. Still, I responded and a conversation ensued.

We talked. We talked for hours.

At first, it was just mundane bullshit: sports, what we did for a living, women.

I was intrigued to find out you're a writer and had a hazy recollection of stocking one of your books; *Confession* I think it was.

I was struck by how much you opened up. And I, in turn, told you about what led me to that point.

"That's some story."

"Well, it's the truth," I explained.

"You should write it down."

"What?"

"Yeah, you should write it all down. It'd make one hell of a book."

I liked the idea. I really liked the idea – me, a writer. And, obviously, I would later follow your advice.

Thanks to you and your suggestion, I had something I really wanted to accomplish – a goal. And I resolved to kick the habit. I would sober up to write my story. I would sober up to tell the world about the love of my life – Prue Baker.

Chapter 22 ◆

The next day, a couple of hours after you were released, they sent me packing – withdraw or not.

That following week and a half was hell – complete and utter hell. The first major blow came on the bus ride back to my apartment.

Sitting there, watching the city pass by, it occurred to me to check my cellphone for messages. There was only one.

"Hey, this is Jess. I hope you're doing alright. I went down to the hospital

and they said you were released. I must
have just missed you. Anyway, I really
need to talk to you. I know we go way
back, and I know you're going through a
lot right now, but I just can't have you
down at the store if you're using drugs.
And I can't afford to pay you if you're not
going to be working. I know it's a shitty
thing to do, but I need to protect my
business. I mean, I have a family to think
about. So... Your last check will be
deposited in your account tomorrow. I
paid you for the whole two-weeks even
though you were only here for a couple of
days." There was a brief pause. "Take
care."

"Son of a bitch," I whispered,
stuffing the phone back in my pocket.

I didn't call him back. What was the
use? He was right. He was right and I
knew it. Still, that didn't stop me from
feeling betrayed.

♦

Back the apartment, I had a situation waiting for me – Alex. As soon as I came through the door, he was all over me.

"Where were you?"

"Hey, Alex. I'll talk to you in a second. Gotta piss."

"In a second? No, motherfucker, you're going to talk to me right now! Right now! Where the fuck where you?!"

"Excuse me? Where the hell do you get off talkin' to me like that? This is still my apartment and, if you don't like it, you can get the fuck out." I responded.

"What the fuck is wrong with you? Leave me here starving, broke, with no food in the house – no idea where you were or what the fuck happened to you. Then you come back with a bad fucking attitude and tell me to get out? And after all I've done for you?!"

"What the fuck have you ever done for me, huh?"

"What have I done? Have me out runnin' around all the time scoring H for you! How's that for starters?!"

"Yeah, and who pays for it?! Who pays for all of it, mine and yours?! Huh?! Who?!"

"You know what? Fuck you. Fuck you," Alex paused, getting right in my face, "Where the fuck were you anyway?"

"Well, if you must know, I was in the hospital," I replied, backing off a bit.

"The hospital?" All at once, Alex seemed much more subdued.

"Yes, I was at the Swedish Medical Center."

"What happened?"

"I ODed."

"What?"

"Yeah, I ODed at work and was rushed to the hospital," Overcome with emotion, I paused briefly. "I almost died. I would've died if Phoebe hadn't found me."

"Oh man, I'm sorry."

"Well, now I think you see why I need you to leave. The drugs, this life, I can't do it anymore."

"That's fine, but what am I supposed to do?"

"You can go stay with your parents. I'm sure they'd let you."

"No. No, there's no fuckin' way I'm staying with my parents."

"Well, then find somewhere else."

"Like where?"

"I don't know."

"You know what? Fuck that! I'm not going anywhere," Alex replied, getting right back in my face.

"The hell you're not!"

"Make me," Alex countered with a shove.

Infuriated, I shoved him back and inadvertently knocked him over the coffee table.

"Oh, it's on now," Alex said, pulling himself up with the sofa.

Immediately, I started towards the kitchen to find a weapon; however, I hardly took two steps when I felt a heavy blow on the back of my head and simultaneously heard a loud musical twang.

It was lights out.

When I finally awoke, I found my guitar lying next to me and the front door was wide open.

Alex was gone and I haven't heard from him since.

♦

In the following days, I was sicker than a dog – couldn't keep anything down. There was the fever, the cold sweats, cramps, and the itching. Christ, the itching. It was unbearable. And, to make matters worse, I was so exhausted. I just couldn't go to sleep.

All that went on, day-after-day, for ten days straight. I thought I was going to die. I wished I was dead.

It was one of the worst experiences of my life. And, worst of all, I realized that it was self-inflicted. It was all self-inflicted. How could I have been so stupid? Heroin? I was addicted to fucking heroin? What the hell is wrong with me?

Chapter 23

Twelve days after being released from the Swedish Medical Center, I was back down at Garrett's Books. No, I didn't go down there to beg for my job back. Fact is, with Prue's life insurance payout, money wasn't a concern. I had enough to live comfortably for a couple of years. Actually, the main reason I went down there was to pick up my car. I wasn't even sure if I'd go inside, but I did.

"Hey, Shane. Did you get my message?" Jess inquired, rushing towards me as I walked through the door.

"Yes, I got your message. I just..."

"Look, if you clean yourself up, I might be able to find a place for you. It's just I can't have you around if you're using drugs." Jess continued, cutting me off.

"Wait. I didn't come down here to ask for my job back."

"Then what is it?"

"I just, umm... I just wanted to apologize. I mean I..."

"Look, you don't need to explain. I know you're going through a lot. Hell, I'm not even sure how you get out of bed. And I would like to help you out, I really would, but I'm not sure what I can do."

"Well, I appreciate it, but there's not really anything you can do," I explained.

"Well, look what the cat drug in. Almost didn't recognize you standing upright," Phoebe mocked as she emerged from the stockroom.

"Phoebe," Jess scolded.

"What?" Phoebe asked with mock innocence.

"Actually Phoebe, I wanted to talk to you too," I stated candidly.

"About what, huh? What do we possibly have to discuss?"

"Well, Phoebe, I wanted to thank you for saving my life."

"Oh, it was nothing. And I mean that."

"Phoebe!" Jess stammered.

And with that, I left.

♦

That night, I was back in the basement of St. James Cathedral. No, not for another Chaste meeting. Sex was the last thing on my mind. Instead, I was there for Addiction Recovery – a support group for people trying to kick the habit and get on with their lives.

I felt welcome. I felt accepted. And,

after I shared my story, I felt something that had eluded me since Prue's death. I felt understood.

I've been back every Friday since.

Chapter 24

Well, here we are at the end. There's not really much left to tell.

About three-weeks after I was released from Swedish Medical Center, I went down to Best Buy and picked up a little ASUS laptop. Actually, I got a really good deal on it because it was still loaded with Windows 7.

Anyway that afternoon, I came back to the apartment, set-up a little work area on the café table in the kitchen, and got to work.

At first, it was really hard. With no

idea what to say or how to begin, I just sat there staring at the screen. I sat there for hours. Occasionally, I'd write something – a sentence or two, but it didn't sound right, so I ended up deleting it.

I never knew writing was so hard.

You made it seem like a piece of cake.

After struggling for about a week with almost nothing to show for my efforts, I was just about to give up. Then it hit me. I should just tell the story like I did when we were in the hospital – only this time with more detail. I'd just write it down rather than say it.

After that, things got a little easier. It was a start. I mean I still ended up sitting there for a long time trying to think of exactly how to tell you the story, but I was making progress.

Sometimes, just to get out of the apartment, I'd take the laptop down to

Starbucks and write. Usually when I did that though, I just ended up sipping a Café Latte, staring out the window, and stealing glances of the cute brunette barista.

All told, it's taken about ten months to get to this point.

Prue's been gone just over a year, but she's still all I think about – morning, noon, and night. Every time I close my eyes, I see her face. Every time I fall asleep, she's in my arms again.

I just need to be with her.

Afterword ♦

Dear Readers,

Shortly after the completion of the story you just read, Shane Nichols sent the manuscript to me, Alan Welker.

As his account dictates, we met during a chance encounter while sharing a room at Swedish Medical Center. I was being held for observation after going into anaphylaxis shock following an incident involving peanuts at the Mariners game earlier that day. Shane was recovering from a heroin overdose which resulted in a near-death-experience.

During our time together in the hospital, Shane and I spoke at length. Most of the conversation revolved around the recent events in his life and the loss of his pregnant fiancée, Prudence Baker.

Being a high school English teacher as well as a prolific author, I immediately recognized the literary potential of his tale and tried to convince him to write his story. Although he seemed a bit skeptical of the idea at first, Shane quickly warmed up to the suggestion. Obviously, he would later follow through and write his story.

I must admit that the arrival of the manuscript was a surprise. Although we exchanged phone numbers in the hospital, we did

not have any further contact. As
for how he received my address, I
am not quite certain, but I
suspect he used an online service.

  After the delivery of the
manuscript, I attempted to contact
Shane, but was unable to reach
him. The following day, while
reading a story entitled "Local
Man Commits Suicide" in the
Seattle Times, I found out why.
It seems Shane returned to the
scene of Prue's accident, in front
of the Central Library, with the
neck of a broken soda bottle.
There, he vertical slit both of
his wrists with the serrated edge.
According to witnesses, Shane then
unscrewed the cap from the neck
and, before collapsing, read a
message aloud, "Your love-life
will be happy and harmonious."
Paramedics would later pronounce

him dead at the scene.

Although I cannot be positive, I am pretty sure that the neck of the broken soda bottle Shane used to inflict his fatal wounds is the same one he recovered from the scene following Prue's traffic accident.

According to what I remember from our conversation and what he mentions in the manuscript, Shane suspected that the broken soda bottle was responsible for the blowout which resulted in Prue's collision with the bus. In essence, it is highly probable that the deaths of both Prue and Shane resulted from the same soda bottle.

A funeral for Shane was held a week later and I was in attendance. As far as funerals go, it was pretty typical up until the graveside service at Mt. Pleasant Cemetery. Shane was to be laid to rest beside the love of his life, Prudence Baker. It was there that I witnessed one of the most extraordinary sights in my life. Just as Shane was being lowered into the ground, the clouds broke, a ray of light shined down right on us, and a rainbow appeared. I know it may not seem like much, but I took it as a sign. Wherever they are, I know they're at peace and they're together.

Regards,

Alan Welker

Alan Welker